Superfairies

Violet the Velvet Rabbit

by Janey Louise Jones

illustrated by Jennie Poh

First published in 2016 by Curious Fox, an imprint of
Capstone Global Library Limited, 264 Banbury Road,
Oxford, OX2 7DY – Registered company number:
6695582

www.curious-fox.com

Text copyright © Janey Louise Jones 2016
Illustrations copyright © Jennie Poh 2016
The author's moral rights are hereby asserted.
All characters in this publication are fictitious
and any resemblance to real persons, living or
dead, is purely coincidental.

ISBN 978 1 78202 347 0
19 18 17 16 15
10 9 8 7 6 5 4 3 2 1

A CIP catalogue for this book is available from the
British Library.

For my sisters, Sticky Toffee and Nana x
– Jennie Poh

Printed and bound in China.

Contents

The Fairy World

The Superfairies of Peaseblossom Woods use teamwork to rescue animals in trouble. They bring together their special superskills, petal power and lots of love.

Superfairy Rose

can blow super healing fairy kisses to make the animals in Peaseblossom Woods feel better.

Superfairy Berry
can see for miles
around with her
super eyesight.

Superfairy Star
can create super dazzling
brightness in one dainty spin
to lighten up dark places.

Superfairy Silk
spins super strong webs
for animal rescues.

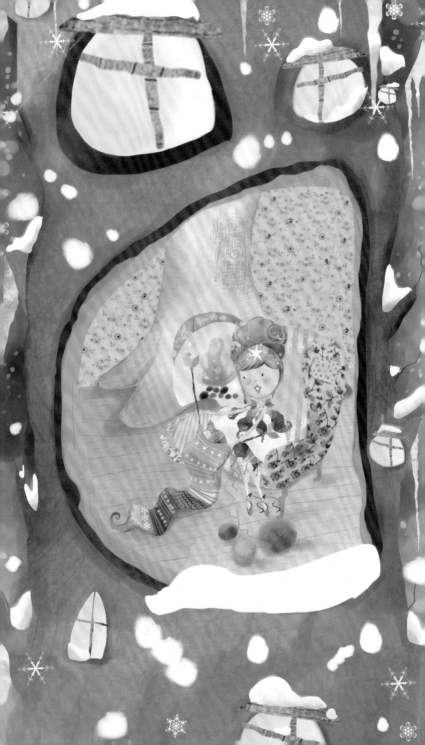

Chapter 1

Snowy Fun

A flurry of soft snow fell over
Peaseblossom Woods. It covered the
landscape like icing sugar on a cake.

It was certainly a cold winter.

Glassy icicles dangled from bare
branches. Twinkly snowflakes clung
to bony twigs. The air was scented by
winter berries and spices.

The Superfairies of the cherry
blossom tree knew the woodland animals
would be cold and hungry.

At this time of year, they took extra
super care of their animal friends.

Inside the Superfairies' cherry blossom tree home, everything was very cosy. A log fire crackled and lanterns glowed. A freshly baked batch of golden honey bread rested on a rack.

Superfairy Star busily knitted hats and scarves for all the young rabbits and squirrels.

The other Superfairies planned the very last feast of the year for all the animals. It would take place in the cherry blossom tree.

Rose read from a menu she had been working on for days. "How does this sound?" she asked.

"Mmmm. Lovely! And let's toast marshmallows on the fire afterwards! And have dancing too!" said Star, who loved to dance.

Lentil & Cinnamon Soup

Honey Bread with Cheese

Mushroom & Walnut Risotto

Sweet Potato Bake

* * *

Lavender Meringues

Almond Iced Star Biscuits

Orange Drizzle Cake

Chocolate Peppermint Creams

"Yes," agreed Silk. "And we'll light candles and hang garlands of holly!"

"Oooh, it's going to be wonderful this year," said Berry. "Let's get to work."

Out in the woods, it snowed steadily until there was more snow than any of the young animals had ever seen before.

Despite the biting cold wind and their rumbling tummies, the little creatures of Peaseblossom Woods thought that playing in the snow was great fun!

Sam Squirrel skated on the frozen lake.

Wheeeee! Bump! It was very slippery! Sam fell over. But up he got!

Martha Mouse caught the falling snow. "Snowflakes are so pretty! I wonder if they really are all different?"

Billy Badger and Basil the Bear Cub
threw snowballs ... of course! "Haha, you
miss me every time, Billy!" teased Basil.

Farrah the Fawn made patterns in the
snow with her feet.

Violet the Velvet Rabbit and Susie Squirrel made skis from wood. Oops, Susie took a tumble! The ground was very uneven under the pretty snow.

Dancer and Cloud, the wild pony sisters, pulled a sledge through the woods.

"Will you join us?" they called out to all the little animals. "We are searching for gifts for the Superfairies as a way of saying thank you for all they do!"

"Coming!" called the young animals.

"The Superfairies are so kind. Let's find them beautiful gifts!" said Violet.

"Yes, what would we do without them?" said Susie.

Chapter 2

Slippery Slope

The young animals all set off to gather gifts with the ponies.

"There are always lovely pine cones as well as pretty snowdrop flowers at the bottom of Snowdrop Slope," said Violet the Velvet Rabbit. "Why don't we go there first?"

"Do you know how to get there?" asked Cloud.

"Oh yes!" said Violet. "I've been there lots of times!"

All the animals followed Violet.

However, things looked a little different when covered by deep snow, and the blizzard was still blowing.

"This way!" called Violet. She waved everyone through the woods, though she did not feel at all confident.

When they came to a crossroads in the woods, Violet was very confused.

"Well," said Farrah, "which way do we go? You said you knew the way!"

"I thought I did," said Violet. "But I'm not completely sure now…"

"Oh dear!" said Martha Mouse. "Does this mean we're lost?"

"We just need to look for the big slope," said Violet. "That's what I normally do."

"But we can't see past our noses," said Susie, "because of all this falling snow."

Susie looked down the possible paths.

Orlando the Owl flew to the top of the trees.

"I think I can see Snowdrop Slope this way," he said.

They all followed his lead.

But Orlando was better at seeing in the dark of night than on a snowy day. After a while, he flew onto a branch, quite exhausted.

"You don't know where we are, do you, Orlando?" said Susie, looking up at him.

"I'm afraid I don't," admitted Orlando.

Violet twitched her nose. She thought she could smell snowdrop flowers.

"I think I know which way to go!" she said. "Everybody, follow me!"

But the animals were nervous about following Violet, because she'd got lost before.

"Please!" said Violet. "Trust me. This time, I really do know where I'm going, I promise!"

"Come on, everyone!" said Susie. "Anyone can get lost once. I believe Violet will find Snowdrop Slope!"

There was a lot of mumbling, but finally everyone agreed to let Violet lead the way.

Violet followed her nose through a dark section of the woods.

"We're almost there," she said.

Once they got through the woods, there was the slope!

"Tada!" said Violet proudly.

At the bottom of the steep slope, they began to collect pine cones for the Superfairies. But Basil found that a bit boring.

"Let's slide down the slope!" he suggested to the others. "I dare you!"

Some of the animals were too scared.

"I'm in lots of trouble already for getting carried away by the wind in autumn," said Martha. "I had better not do anything silly."

"Scaredy!" said Basil. "Violet, are you too frightened as well?"

"No!" said Violet boldly. "I'll do it! Nothing scares me."

"Are you sure about this?" asked Martha. "Wouldn't you prefer to stay and just watch Basil whizz down?"

"No, he's not the only brave one round here," said Violet. "I'll take my skis. Wish me luck!"

Martha looked worried. "Good luck, Violet. You're so brave," she said.

So Basil and Violet climbed their way to the top of Snowdrop Slope.

"Oh no!" said Violet as she looked down the slope. "What a long way down!"

"I'm not even going to think about it!" said Basil. "You follow me down. Wait until a few minutes after I've left. See you at the bottom!"

"Could we hold hands and go down together?" asked Violet.

"No, we might bump into each other," said Basil. "And anyway, you have the skis. Don't give up now, Violet. You are so cool for coming up here. You can do it!"

Basil launched himself fearlessly down the hill.

Glee!

Wheeee!

Whoosh!

"This is brilliant fun!" called Basil.
"I've never gone so fast!"

"I'm going to try it now!" announced the Velvet Rabbit bravely, getting her skis into position.

"Don't do it!" called Martha.

"Crawl down carefully!" cried Susie.

For a few moments, it looked like Violet was in two minds, but then she made up her mind to … goooooooooo!

"Aaargh!" she cried, as she slipped down the slope, falling on her bottom. Her skis and poles went flying in the air.

Violet raced down as fast as a snowball.

"Help!" she cried. "I don't like this! Help me!"

Oh no! The slope was so slippery, she went faster and faster.

At last, she came to a sudden stop at a sharp ledge of snow. She hung on to the ledge, dangling over a deep valley below.

"Rescue me!" she cried. "Somebody, please! My paws are so cold … I can't hold on here for much longer."

Chapter 3

Violet's Big Splash

The log fire danced merrily in the fireplace of the Superfairies' sitting room. The woolly hats were all knitted, while the toasty winter feast was ready at last!

Ting-aling-aling…

Ting-aling-aling…

The warning bells began to tinkle.

"Oh dear! The animals need us!" said Star. "I was so afraid something might happen in this dreadful weather."

"I couldn't bear for anyone to be hurt," said Rose. "Superfairies! Action!"

The Superfairies pulled their fluffy winter wraps around them and put on their floral wellies. They picked up the warming feather cloak and flew out to the fairycopter.

Rose quickly checked the Strawberry computer.

"What can you see?" asked Silk.

"It's showing Violet the Velvet Rabbit hanging on to a ledge of snow! She must be freezing!" said Rose.

"I can hardly see with the falling snow. I'll do my best. 5, 4, 3, 2, 1 ... go, go, go!" said Berry.

The fairycopter lifted up into the snowy winter sky.

When they landed at Snowdrop Slope, the little animals were huddled together, fretting about Violet the Velvet Rabbit.

The Superfairies looked up to the ledge where Violet was in peril.

"Wait there, Violet," called Rose looking up to the top of the slope. "We're on our way!"

"Thank you!" called the Velvet Rabbit. "I'm really scared! And my paws are about to let go!"

The Superfairies set off to fetch her.

But Violet's voice rolling down the hill seemed to have made the snow under her rumble.

There was some rippling movement in the snow, and a low, thundery sound grumbled in the air.

A great mass of snow began to roll downhill. The tiny rabbit was caught up in the middle of it. She tumbled down the slope, carried along by the fast moving snow.

"Help me!" she cried, her voice muffled by the rush of snow around her. "I can't stop!"

The Superfairies flew above her, following the little Velvet Rabbit's speedy progress down the slippery slope.

Rose tried to stop the snowball with a healing kiss, but the kiss missed. The snowball was going too fast!

Silk dropped a ladder, but Violet could not grab it.

Star and Berry were able to get closer to Violet, but she was covered in too much snow for them to grab her.

At the base of the slope, Violet bumped against a tree trunk lying flat along the ground, and was promptly thrown high into the air, flying in a curve.

Where would she land?

The Superfairies followed her anxiously.

All the young animals ran towards her as she started to drop down. She was getting lower …

and lower …

and lower.

Smack! Crack! She landed on the middle of a frozen pond.

The Superfairies dashed to the scene while the animals waited at the water's edge.

"Stay still, Violet!" called Silk from above. "The ice is very thin…"

"It's not that thin," said Violet, feeling excited about being so close to safety. "I can make it to land!"

"Please don't move!" called Rose.

But Violet was too excited and began to bunny-hop across the pond.

Bounce,

bounce,

bounce,

crack!

Oh no!

The ice around Violet broke up and—

Splash! She fell into the freezing pond below!

"Aaargh!" cried Violet. "It's so cold! It's horrid! I want Mummy and Daddy!"

Above Violet, the Superfairies got into a huddle to plan how to help her.

The little bunny bobbed around in a dark watery hole in the ice.

Chapter 4

The Winter Feast

Star dazzled the water with brightness so they could see her clearly.

Twinkle. Sparkle. Dazzle. Tada!

"That's better!" said Silk.

"Now go in for her!" said Rose.

Silk and Berry swooped in towards Violet at top speed, while Star hovered as back-up.

They reached down for her, plucking her freezing little body from the icy pond in one move.

The Superfairies' arms didn't look strong enough to carry the little rabbit across the pond. But luckily the Superfairies are super strong.

"Hurrah!" cried all the animals, as the Superfairies wrapped a shivering Violet in the warming feather cloak.

Rose blew lots of healing kisses.

Violet gave a great shudder. Then a huge shiver. Followed by a little giggle.

"I think I'm going to be fine!" she said.

The Superfairies smiled with relief, but they had to talk to Violet about what she had done.

"You know it was very silly to go to the top of the slope," said Berry.

"I'm sorry," said Violet. She didn't want to tell the Superfairies that Basil had encouraged her.

However, Basil felt guilty. "It was my fault," he blurted out. "I said Violet would be a scaredy if she didn't come up to the top!"

Rose looked very disappointed, which made Basil feel terrible.

"Violet could have been very seriously hurt," said Rose. "And so could you. This could have spoiled the whole Winter Feast."

"I know," said Basil. "I won't do anything like that again! I promise."

"Make sure you don't," said Rose. "Let's forget it for now, but be more careful in future."

The Superfairies flew Violet in the fairycopter back to the cherry blossom tree for the Winter Feast.

The other animals arrived on the sledge, pulled by Dancer and Cloud, with the older family members following on.

"Let's decorate the cherry blossom tree now for the Superfairies!" said Cloud.

"Oh, thank you," said Rose.

The animals strung garlands of berries and pine cones across the tree house. They placed holly and ivy along the fireplaces, and left gifts of nuts and dried fruits.

The woodland friends ate the delicious
Winter Feast given by the Superfairies
and sang songs around the toasty log fire.

After that, the animals snuggled up
together for a big sleepover.

The next day, the animals had to go back to their own homes for the long winter sleep.

"Bye, Superfairies. Thanks for everything!" called the animals.

The Superfairies gathered round the fire, nibbling on tasty leftovers from the feast.

"Phew, it's been quite a day," said Star.

"Quite a year, actually!" agreed Berry. "Our rescue skills have been well tested."

"At least the animals can't get into trouble when they're asleep!" said Silk.

"That's true," said Rose. "But we will miss them so much!"

"Yes, but before we know it, spring will be here!" said Star. "We can look forward to that!"

"Yes," said Rose. "But until then, let's stay cosy together!"

"Why don't we dance to celebrate a good year of rescues!" said Star.

The other Superfairies giggled. Star liked to dance whenever she could!

The Superfairies held hands and danced inside the cherry blossom tree.

Fairies from the blossom tree,
Superskills galore have we.

Caring in this charming wood
For needy animals, as we should.

Twinkle, sparkle, dazzle, swish,
Tending animals as they wish.

And when a rescue's nicely done,
It's time to have some fairy fun.

Dancing, singing, twirling, glee,
All around our blossom tree!

All About Fairies

The legend of fairies is as old as time. Fairy tales tell stories of fairy magic. According to legend, fairies are so small and delicate, and fly so fast, that they might actually be all around us, but just very hard to see. Fairies, supposedly, only reveal themselves to believers.

Fairies often dance in circles at sunrise and sunset. They love to play in woodlands among wildflowers. If you sing gently to them, they may very well appear.

Here are some of the world's most famous fairies:

The Flower Fairies

Artist Cicely Mary Barker painted a range of pretty flower fairies and published eight volumes of flower fairy art from 1923. The link between fairies and flowers is very strong.

The Tooth Fairy

She visits us during the night to leave a coin when we lose our baby teeth. Although it is very hard to catch sight of her, children are always happy when she visits.

Fake Fairies

In 1917, cousins Elsie Wright and Frances Griffiths said they photographed fairies in their garden. They later admitted that most were fakes – but Frances claimed that one was genuine.

Which Superfairy Are You?

1. What is your favourite musical instrument?
   A) violin
   B) flute
   C) trumpet
   D) piano

2. Do you dream about:
   A) holidays
   B) wildflower meadows
   C) summer picnics
   D) being on the stage

3. For a day out, would you prefer:
   A) to take a boat trip
   B) to visit friends
   C) to attend a sports event
   D) to go shopping

4. Which of these girls' names do you prefer?
   A) Sasha
   B) Daisy
   C) Polly
   D) Angel

5. What is your ideal pet?
   A) kitten
   B) puppy
   C) rabbit
   D) pony

6. Which holiday sounds nicest?
   A) a trip to the beach
   B) relaxing at a country cottage
   C) going camping
   D) staying at a luxury hotel

7. What do you prefer to play with?
   A) skipping rope
   B) teddy or soft toy
   C) ball
   D) doll

8. Which word sums you up best?
   A) fun-loving
   B) gentle
   C) helpful
   D) entertaining

Mostly A – you are like Silk – adventurous and brave, you always think of ways to deal with problems! You enjoy action and adventures.

Mostly B – you are like Rose – gentle, kind and loving. You are good at staying calm and love pink things.

Mostly C – you are like Berry – good fun, always helpful, with lots of great ideas. You are sensible and wise.

Mostly D – you are like Star – you cheer people up and dazzle with your sparkling ways! You are funny and enjoy jokes and dancing.

About the Author

Janey Louise Jones has been a published author for 10 years. Her *Princess Poppy* series is an international bestselling brand, with books translated into 10 languages, including Hebrew and Mandarin. Janey is a graduate of Edinburgh University and lives in Edinburgh with her three sons. She loves fairies, princesses, beaches and woodlands.

About the Illustrator

Jennie Poh was born in England and grew up in Malaysia (in the jungle). At the age of 10 she moved back to England and trained as a ballet dancer. She studied fine art at Surrey Institute of Art & Design as well as fashion illustration at Central Saint Martins. Jennie loves the countryside, animals, tea and reading. She lives in Woking with her husband and two wonderful daughters.

THE *Fun* DOESN'T STOP HERE!

JOIN THE SUPERFAIRES ON MORE
MAGICAL ANIMAL RESCUES!

Basil the Bear Cub
by Janey Louise Jones

Dancer the Wild Pony
by Janey Louise Jones

Martha the Little Mouse
by Janey Louise Jones

Violet the Velvet Rabbit
by Janey Louise Jones

For more exciting books from
brilliant authors, follow the fox!

www.curious-fox.com